Frederic Ouvry, Thomas W. Newton

Catalogue of Old Ballads

Frederic Ouvry, Thomas W. Newton

Catalogue of Old Ballads

ISBN/EAN: 9783744777087

Printed in Europe, USA, Canada, Australia, Japan

Cover: Foto ©Andreas Hilbeck / pixelio.de

More available books at **www.hansebooks.com**

Catalogue

OF

OLD BALLADS

IN THE POSSESSION OF

FREDERIC OUVRY, Esq.,

PRESIDENT OF THE SOCIETY OF ANTIQUARIES.

COMPILED BY

T. W. NEWTON,

F. R. HIST. SOC., ASSISTANT LIBRARIAN OF THE
ROYAL SCHOOL OF MINES.

London:

PRIVATELY PRINTED.

LONDON:
PRINTED BY THOMAS SCOTT, WARWICK COURT,
HOLBORN.

INDEX.

NOTE.—This Index includes the SUBJECTS OF THE BALLADS, AUTHORS, FIRST LINES AND CHORUSES, PRINTERS AND PUBLISHERS, and TUNES.

CATALOGUE.

Old Ballads.

1.—Two proper nue Balletes.

    I.   *E. hath my herte in holde.*

    II.   *A thousand times I me recomende.*

             (**Black letter.** No date.)

                              [*Vol.* i. *p.* 1.

2.—The prayer of the Prophet Daniel wrytten in the ix. chapter of his Prophecie no leſſe Godly then neceſſary for all men at this preſent. (Imperfect.)

    O Lord that art our God, &c.

          Imprinted at London, in Temestrete, by Hughe
          Syngelton, at the sygne of the dobble hood,
          ouer agaynst the Stylyard (**Black letter.**
          No date.)

                          [*Vol.* i. *p.* 2.

B

3.—A prayer, and alfo a thankefgiuing vnto God, for his great mercy, in giuing, and preferuing our Noble Queene Elizabeth, to liue and reigne ouer vs, to his honour and glory, and our comfort in Chrift Iefus, to be fung the xvii. day of Nouember 1577. Made by I. Pitt, minifter.

Be light, and glad, in God rejoyce, &c.

Imprinted by Christopher Barkar. (**Black letter. No date.**)

[*Vol. i. p. 3.*

4.—The Lamentation of Englande: For the late Treafons confpired againft the Queenes Maieftie and the whole Realme, by Franuees (*sic*) Throgmorton: who was executed for the fame at Tyborne, on Friday being the tenth day of July laft paft, 1584.

To the tune of Weepe, weepe.

With brinishe teares and sobbing sighes.

Pray pray, and praise the Lord (chorus).

W. M.

Imprinted at London, by Richard Ihones. (**Black letter. No date.**)

[*Vol. i. p. 4.*

5.—A proper new Ballad, breefely declaring the Death and Execution of 14 moft wicked Traitors, who fuffered death in Lincolnes Inne feelde neere London the 20 and 21 of September 1586. (With fourteen portraits :— 1. John Ballard, Preeft; 2. Anthony Babington; 3. John Sauage; 4. Robert Barnwell; 5. Chodicus

Techburne ; 6. Charles Tilney ; 7. Edward
Abbington ; 8. Thomas Salfbury ; 9. Henry Dun ;
10. Edward Ihones ; 11. John Trauers ; 12. John
Charnock ; 13. Robert Gage ; 14. Harman Bellamy.)

To the tune of Weep, weep.

Rejoyce in hart good people all.

O praise the Lord with hart and minde (chorus).

T. D.

Imprinted at London at the Long Shop adioyning
vnto Saint Mildreds Churche in the Pultrie by
Edward Alde. (**Black letter.** No date.)

[*Vol. i. p. 5*

6.—A warning to all falfe Traitors by example of 14, wherof
vi. were executed in diuers places neere about London,
and 2 neere Braintford the 28 day of Auguft, 1588.
Alfo at Tyborne were executed the 30 day vi.,
namely 5 Men and one Woman. (With fourteen
portraits :—1. William Deane ; 2. Henry Webley ;
3. William Gunter ; 4. Robert Moorton ; 5 Hugh
Moore ; 6. Thomas Acton ; 7. Thomas Felton ;
8. James Clarkfon ; 9. Richard Flewett ; 10. Edward
Shelley ; 11. Richard Leigh ; 12. Richard Martin ;
13. John Rooche ; 14. Margeret Ward.)

To the tune of Green-fleeues.

You Traitors all that doo deuise.

Imprinted at London by Edward Alde. (**Black
letter.** No date.)

[*Vol. i. p. 6*

7.—The wonderfull example of God shewed vpon Iasper
    Coningham, a gentleman borne in Scotland, who was
    of oppinion that there was neither God nor Diuell,
    Heauen nor Hell.

> To the tune of O neighbour Robert.
>
> *It was a Scotchman.*
>
> Imprinted at London for Thomas Millington, and
> are to be solde at his shop in Cornehill. (**Black
> letter.** No date.)
>
> [*Vol.* i. *p.* 7.

8.—The Lamentation of Mr. Page's Wife of Plimouth, who
    being forc'd to Wed him, consented to his Murder,
    for the Love of G. Strangwidge, for which they
    suffered at Barnstable, in Devonshire.

> The tune, Fortune my Foe.
>
> *Unhappy she whom fortune hath forlorn.*
>
> (No date.)   [*Vol.* i. *p.* 8.

9.—The Lamentation of George Strangwidge, who for the
    consenting to the death of Mr. Page of Plymouth,
    suffered death at Barstable. [Also,] The Complaint
    of Ulallia, for the causing her Husband to be
    murdered for the love of Strangwidge, who were
    executed together. (Two ballads.)

> I. *The man that sighs and sorrows for his sin.*
>
> II. *If eer one did touch a woman's heart.*
>
> (No date.)   [*Vol.* i. *p.* 9.

10.—The Louers complaint for the loffe of his Loue.   (With illuftration.)

To a pleasant new tune.

I wander up and downe.

Printed by the Assignes of Thomas Symcocke.
(Black letter. No date.)

[*Vol.* i. *p.* 10.

11.—A pleafant new Ballad of two Louers.   (With illuftrations.)

To a pleasant new tune.

Complaine my Lute, complaine on him.

Printed by the Assignes of Thomas Symcock.
(Black letter. No date.)

[*Vol.* i. *p.* 11.

12.—In this Table is fet forth three principall things : Firft mans Creation : fecondly, his Mifery in Adams Fall : and laftly, the happy reftoring againe of all the faithfull by Chrift to the vnchangeable loue of God. A Table fit for all Chriftians to know.   (With illuftrations.)

Almightie God made by his Word.

I. D.

Printed at London for Thomas Ellis at the signe of the Christopher in Paul's Churchyard, 1629.
(Black letter.)

[*Vol.* i. *p.* 12.

13.—The Country-mans New Care away. (With illuftrations.)

To the tune of Love will find out the way.

If there were imployments.

The Second Part. To the same tune.

If Children to Parents.

RO. GUY.

London : Printed for H. Gosson. (Black letter. No date.)

[*Vol.* i. *p.* 13.

14.—The defperate Damfells Tragedy ; or, the faithleffe young man. (With illuftrations.)

To the tune of Dulcina.

In the gallant month of June.

The Second Part. To the same tune.

You Gods (quoth she) I invocate.

M. P.

London : Printed for H. G. (Black letter. No date.)

[*Vol.* i. *p.* 15, 16.

15.—The Conftant Lover. (With illuftrations.)

To a Northerne tune called, Shall the absence of my Mistresse.

You loyall Lovers that are distant.

The Second Part. To the same tune.

I to her will be like Leander.

P. L.

London : Printed for Henry Gosson. (Black letter. No date.)

[*Vol.* i. *p.* 17, 18.

16.—A new Love-Song, and a true Love-Song. (With illuftrations.)

To the tune of Colin and Amarillis.

Loyal Lovers listen well.

The Second Part. To the same tune.

Oh dear Love be you content.

THOMAS JONES.

London: Printed for Richard Burton, at the Horfhoue in Smithfield. (**Black letter.** No date.)

[*Vol.* i. *p.* 19, 20.

17.—A pleafant new Northerne Song, called the two York-fhire Louers. (With illuftrations.)

To a pleafant new Court tune; or, the tune of Willy.

When Willy once he stayed.

The Second Part. To the same tune.

White Lilies shall pave the closes.

Printed at London for I. W. (**Black letter.** No date.)

[*Vol.* i. *p.* 21, 22.

18.—The Honor of the Inns of Court Gentlemen; or, a briefe recitall of the Magnificent and matchleffe fhow, that paft from Hatton and Ely houfe in Holborne to White-hall on Monday night, being the third of February, and the next day after Candlemas. (With illuftrations.)

To the tune of Our noble King in his Progreffe.

My noble Mase assist me.

The Second Part. To the same tune.

But that which admiration.

To the honor of those Gentry that live at the Inns of Court (chorus).

M. P.

London: Printed for Thomas Lambert. (**Black letter.** No date.)

[*Vol.* i. *p.* 23, 24.

19.—The Mad Mans Morrice.   (With illuftrations.)

To a pleasant new tune.

Heard you not lately of a man.

The Second Part. To the same tune.

Then raging towards the Skie I rose.

HUMFREY CROWCH.

London: Printed for Richard Harper in Smithfield. (**Black letter.** No date.)

[*Vol.* i. *p.* 25, 26.

20.—New Mad Tom of Bedlam ; or,
        The Man in the Moon drinks Claret,
        With Powder-beef, Turnep and Carret.
                        (With illuftrations.)

Tune is, Grays-In-Mask.

Forth from my sad and darksome Cell.

(**Black letter.** No date.)

[*Vol.* i. *p.* 27.

21.—The Man in the Moon Drinks Clarret. As it was lately Sung at the Curtain, Holy-Well. (With illuſtration.)

To the same tune.

Bacchus the Father of drunken Nowls.

Printed for W. Thackeray and T. Paſſinger. (**Black letter.** No date.)

[*Vol.* i. *p.* 28.

22.—The Lamenting Ladies [viz. The Lady Elizabeth, Daughter to Charles I.] farewel to the world, who being in ſtrange Exile, bewails her own Miſery, complains upon Fortune and Deſtiny, deſcribes the manner of her Breeding ; deplores the loſs of her Parents, wiſhing Peace and Happineſs to England, which was their Native Country : And withal, reſolved for Death, chearfully recommended her Soul to Heaven, and her Body to earth, and quietly departed this Life, Anno 1650.

To an excellent new tune, called Oh hone, oh hone.

Mournful Melpomenie assist my Quil.

The Second Part. To the same tune.

My Garments drest with pearl.

(No date.)

[*Vol.* i. *p.* 29.

23.—A Spirituall Song of Comfort, or Incouragement to the Souldiers that now are gone forth in the Cauſe of Chriſt. With four portraits :—1. The Earl

C

Essex ; 2. The E. of Warwick ; 3. Sir Wil. Waller ;
4. Mr. Pym.)

Come along my valiant Souldiers.

WILLIAM STARBUCKE.

Printed in the yeere wherein Antichrist is falling.
(No date.)

[*Vol.* i. *p.* 30.

24.—The four-legg'd Elder ; or, a horrible Relation of a Dog,
and an Elders Maid.   (Imperfect.)

To the tune of The Lady's fall.

All Christians and Lay-Elders too.

O house of Commons, house of Peeres (chorus).

(No date.)

[*Vol.* i. *p.* 31.

25.—Mad Tom a Bedlams defires of peace ; or, his Benedicities
for diftracted Englands reftauration to her wits again.
By a conftant, though unjuft, fufferer (now in prifon)
for his Majefties juft Regality, and his Countreys
Liberty.   S F W B.

Poor Tom hath been imprison'd.

Printed : Anno Domini, 1648.

[*Vol.* i. *p.* 32.

26.—The Rump Carbonadod ; or, a New Ballad.

To the tune of The Black-smith.

Lend me your ears, not cropt, and I'le sing.

Which no body can deny (chorus).

(Black letter chiefly.   No date.)

[*Vol.* i. *p.* 33.

27.—November.

Thou Sun that shed'st the Dayes, looke downe and see.

(No date.)

[*Vol.* i. *p.* 34.

28.—England's Black Tribunal; or, King Chrales's (*sic*) Martyrdom. (With illuftration.)

True Churchmen all, I pray behold & see.

London: Printed and sold by R. Coster, at No. 14, Hosier-Lane, West-Smithfield. (No date.)

[*Vol.* i. *p.* 35.

29.—(No Title. Relates to Charles II.)

Our age strange things hath brought to light.

The Second Part. To the same tune.

Then shall we hear sweet harmony.

A second Charles once more shall Reign (chorus).

J. W.

London: Printed for John Andrews, at the White Lion, near Pye Corner. (Black letter chiefly. No date.)

[*Vol.* i. *p.* 36, 37.

30.—(No Title, or Firft Part. Relates to the fame fubject as the foregoing.)

The Second Part. To the same tune.

The Citizens brave.

London: Printed for John Andrews, at the White Lyon. (Black letter. No date.)

[*Vol.* i. *p.* 38.

31.—(No Title. Execution of a cruel Wife. Allufion made to Robert Willmot.)

Unto the Lord that rules above.

London: Printed for John Andrews, at the white Lion, near Pye-Corner. (**Black letter.** No date.)

[*Vol.* i. *p.* 36*.

32.—The Examination, Confeffion, and Execution of Urfula Corbet, who, for Poyfoning of her Hufband Simon Corbet, was Burned near to Worcefter the fifteenth day of March, 1660. (With illuftrations.)

To the tune of The bleeding Heart.

Good women all, a while give ear.

(**Black letter.** No date.)

[*Vol.* i. *p.* 39.

33.—I Warrant thee Boy, Shee's Right ; or, an exact Character of a Wanton Lafs.

To a very rare Northern tune ; or, All Hail to the dayes.

Come hither young Sinner.

I'll warrant thee Boy, shee's Right (chorus).

London : Printed for Tho. Vere, at the sign of the Angell, without Newgate. 1661.

[*Vol.* i. *p.* 40.

34.—A New Ballad of a famous German Prince and a renowned Englifh Duke, who on St. James's day One thoufand 666 fought with a Beaft with Seven Heads, call'd Provinces; not by Land, but by Water; not to be faid, but fung; not in high Englifh nor Low Dutch; but

To a new French tune, call'd Monsieur Ragou; or, The Dancing Hobby-horses.

There happen'd of late a terrible Fray.

With a Thump, Thump, Thump (chorus).

London: Printed by James Cotterel, in the year 1666.

[Vol. i. p. 11.

35.—A Dialogue between the D. of C. and the D. of P., at their meeting in Paris, with the Ghoft of Jane Shore.

Art thou return'd, my sister Concubine.

London: Printed for J. Smith. (No date.)

[Vol. i. p. 42—45.

36.—Bloody News from Chelmsford; or, a Proper New Ballad, containing a true and perfect Relation of a moft barbarous Murther committed upon the Body of a Country Parfon, who died of a great Wound given him in the Bottom of his Belly, by a moft Cruel Country-Butcher, for being too familiar with his Wife: For which Fact he is to be Tried for his Life at this next Afhizes.

To the tune of Chevy-Chase.

Give o'er, ye chiming ranting Lads.

Oxford: Printed in the year MDCLXIII.

[*Vol.* i. *p.* 16.

37.—Newes from Hide-Parke; or, a very merry paſſage which happened betwixt a North Country Gentleman and a very Gaudy Gallant Lady of pleaſure, whom he took up in the Parke, and conducted her (in her own Coach) home to her Lodgings, and what chanced there, if you'l venture Attention the Song will declare. (With illuſtrations.)

To the tune of The Croſt Couple.

One evening, a little before it was dark.

Tan-tivvee (chorus).

London: Printed for William Gilbertſon dwelling in Giltſpur-ſtreet. (**Black letter.** No date.)

[*Vol.* i. *p.* 47.

38.—The Common Cries of London Town, Some go up ſtreet, ſome go down.

With Turners Diſh of Stuff, or a Gallymaufery. (With illuſtration.)

To the tune of Watton Towns End.

My Masters all attend you.

The Second Part. To the same tune.

That's the fat foole of the Curtin.

W. TURNER.

London: Printed for F. C., T. V., and W. G., 1662. (**Black letter.**)

[*Vol.* i. *p.* 18, 19.

39.—The Tryall of True love to you I will Recite,
Between a fair young lady and a courteous knight.
(With illuftrations.)

The tune is, Dainty come thou to me.

Dear Love regard my grief.

Printed for F. Coles, T. Vere, W. Gilbertson.
(**Black letter.** No date.)

[*Vol.* i. *p.* 50, 51.

40.—The Gowlin; or, a Pleafant Fancy for the Spring; being
an Encounter betwixt a Scotch Leard & a buxome
begger-wench. (With illuftrations.)

To a new Play house tune; or, See the Gowlin, &c.

Abroad as I was walking.

To see the Gowlin (chorus).

Printed for I. Wright, I. Clark, W. Thackeray, and
T. Passinger. (**Black letter.** No date.)

[*Vol.* i. *p.* 52.

41.—The Souldiers Farewel to his love; being a Dialogue
betwixt Thomas and Margaret. (With illuftration.)

To a pleasant new tune.

Margaret my sweetest, Margaret I must go.

London: Printed for F. Coles, T. Vere, and
J. Wright. (**Black letter.** No date.)

[*Vol.* i. *p.* 53.

42.—The Wanton Wife of Baith.

To the tune of Flying Fame.

In Baith a wanton wife did dwell.

(No date.)

[*Vol.* i. *p.* 54.

43.—An Excellent Ballad of the Mercers Son of Midhurst and the Cloathiers Daughter of Guilford.

To the tune of, Dainty come thou to me.

There was a wealthy man.

(Black letter. No date.)

[*Vol.* i. *p.* 55.

44.—A Ballad, intituled, The Old Mans Complaint againſt his Wretched Son, who, to Advance his Marriage, did undo himſelf. (With illuſtrations.)

To the same tune.

All you that Fathers be.

J. M. and A. M.

Printed for and sold by W. Thackeray, at the Angel in Duck Lane. (Black letter. No date.)

[*Vol.* i. *p.* 56.

45.—An Excellent Ballad of Noble Marqueſs and Patient Griſſel. (With illuſtration.)

To the tune of The Brides Good-morrow.

A Noble Marquess.

Printed by and for Alex. Milbourn, in Green-Arbor Court in the Little-Old-Baily. (Black letter. No date.)

[*Vol.* i. *p.* 57. 58.

46.—The Courteous Carman, and the Amorous Maid; or, the Carman's Whiftle. (With illuftrations.)

To the tune of The Carman's Whistle; or, Lord Willoughby's March.

As I abroad was walking.

London: Printed by and for W. O., and are to be sold by C. Bates, in Pye-corner. (**Black letter.** No date.)

[*Vol.* i. *p.* 59.

47.—A New Ballad of King John and the Abbot of Canterbury. (With illuftrations.)

To the tune of The King and the Lord Abbot.

I'll tell you a Story, a Story anon.

Printed for P. Brooksby, at the Golden Ball in Pye-corner. (**Black letter.** No date.)

[*Vol.* i. *p.* 60.

48.—The Winchefter Wedding; or, Ralph of Reading and Black Befs of the Green. (With illuftrations.)

To a new Country Dance; or, The King's Jigg.

At Winchester was a Wedding.

London: Printed for J. Deacon, at the Angel in Guilt-spur-street, without Newgate. (**Black letter.** No date.)

[*Vol.* i. *p.* 61.

49.—The Life and Death of the Famous Thomas Stukely, an Englifh Gallant in time of Queen Elizabeth, who ended his Life in a Battel of three Kings of Barbary. (With illuftration.)

Tune is, King Henry's going to Bulloign.

In the West of England.

Printed by and for T. Norris and C. Brown, and sold at the Looking-glass on London-bridge. (No date.)

[*Vol.* i. *p.* 62.

50.—The true Loves Knot untyed; being the right path, whereby to advife Princely Virgins how to behave themfelves, by the example of the renouned Princefs, the Lady Arabella, and the fecond Son to the Lord Seymore, late Earl of Hertford. (With illuftration.)

To the tune of Frogs Galiards.

As I from Ireland did pass.

(**Black letter**. No date. Ten verses only.)

[*Vol.* i. *p.* 63.

51.—(The fame Ballad in full.)

To the same tune.

As I to Ireland did pass.

London : Printed by and for C. Brown and T. Norris, and sold at the Looking-glass on London-bridge. (No date.)

[*Vol.* i. *p.* 64.

52.—The Thames Uncas'd; or, the Watermans Song upon the Thaw.

To the tune of Hey Boys up go we.

Come, ye merry men all.

London. Printed for the Author, and sold by J. Norris at the Kings Arms without Temple-bar, 1684.

[*Vol.* i. *p.* 65.

53.—Virtue and Beauty in Danger; or, King Edward's Courting the London Virgin. (With illustrations.)

Fair angel of England, thy beauty most bright.

(No date.)

[*Vol.* i. *p.* 66.

54.—Poor Robin's Dream; commonly called Poor Charity. (With illustrations.)

To a complete tune, well known by Musicians, and many others; or, A Game at Cards.

How now, good fellow, what all amort?

(No date.)

[*Vol.* i. *p.* 67.

55.—A lamentable Ballad of the Tragical End of a Gallant Lord and his Beautiful Lady, with the untimely Death of their Children, wickedly performed by a Heathen Blackamore, their Servant: The like seldom heard before. (With illustration.)

In Rome a Nobleman did wed.

No date.

Vol. i. p. 68.

56.—A Famous Sea-Fight, between Captain Ward and the
Rainbow. (With illuſtration.)

Strike up, you lusty gallants.

(No date.)

[*Vol. i. p.* 69.

57.—The Jolly Gentleman's Frolick; or, the City Ramble.
Being an Account of a young Gallant, who Wager'd
to paſs any of the Watches, without giving them an
Anſwer; but beirg ſtopp'd by the Conſtable at
Cripple-gate, was ſent to the Counter, afterwards had
before my Lord-Mayor, and was clear'd by the
Interceſſion of my Lord-Mayor's Daughter. (With
illuſtrations.)

To a pleaſant new tune.

Give ear to a Frolicksome Ditty.

London: Printed for C. Bates, at the Sun and
Bible in Gilt-ſpur-ſtreet, near Pye. . . .
(No date.)

[*Vol. i. p.* 70.

58.—An Excellent Ballad, intitul'd, The Unfortunate Love of
a Lancaſhire Gentleman, and the hard Fortune of a
fair young Bride. (With illuſtrations.)

To the tune of Come follow my Love.

Look you faithful lovers.

Alack for my Love I shall dye (chorus).

London: Printed by and for T. Norris, at the
Looking glass on London bridge. (No date.)

[*Vol. i. p.* 71.

59.—Blanket-Fair; or, the Hiftory of Temple Street. Being a Relation of the merry Pranks plaid on the River Thames during the great Froft.

To the tune of Packington's Pound.

Come liften awhile (though the Weather be cold).

Printed for Charles Corbet, at the Oxford Arms in Warwick Lane, 1684.

[*Vol.* i. *p.* 72.

60.—Thamafis's Advice to the Painter, from her Frigid Zone; or, Wonders upon the Water.

Fam'd Thamasis, with shiv'ring Winter Dresses.

London: Printed by G. Croom, on the River of Thames. (No date.)

[*Vol.* i. *p.* 73, 74.

61.—Froft Fair. (View of the Thames.)

Behold the liquid Thames now frozen o'er.

Printed upon the Ice, on the River Thames, Jan. 23d, 1739/40.

[*Vol.* i. *p.* 75.

62.—The Mad Man's Morice; or,
            A Warning for young men to have a care,
            How they in love intangled are.
                        (With illuftrations.)

To a pleasant new tune.

Heard you not lately of a man.

Printed by and for A. M., and sold by the Booksellers of London. (No date.)

[*Vol.* i. *p.* 76.

63.—The Doleful Lamentation of Thomas Dangerfield, who was lately apprehended and imprisoned in Newgate, for High Misdemeanor, &c.

To the tune of 'Tis for mine own offence I must Dye.

Mark well my words, you Country Men.

London: Printed for J. Huzzey, 1685.

[*Vol.* i. *p.* 77.

64.—The Glory of the West; or, the Virgins of Taunton Dean, who ript open their Silk-Petticoats, to make Colours for the late D. of M.'s Army, when he came before the Town. A Song.

To the tune of The Winchester Wedding.

In Lime began a Rebellion.

London: Printed for James Dean, Bookseller at the Queens Head between the Royal Grove and Helmet in Drury-Lane, 1685.

[*Vol.* i. *p.* 78.

65.— . . . . London's Petition . . . their . . . Parliament of old Women . . . threescore thousand Hands, and . . . ad nor Widow amongst them. (With illustrations. Imperfect.)

. . . . . of Mary live long.

You Matrons all.

Printed for Josiah Blare, at the Looking-Glass on London-Bridge. (Black letter. No date. See No. 77.)

[*Vol.* i. *p.* 79.

66.—The Beggars Chorus, in the Jovial Crew. (With illuſtrations.)

To an excellent new tune.

There was a Jovial Beggar.

And a Begging we will go (chorus).

Printed for J. Walter, at the Golden Ball in Pyecorner. (No date.)

[*Vol.* i. *p.* 80.

67.—A Provd and Blaſphemovs Cahllenge (*sic*), given out in denuntiation of warre, by Amurath the great Turk, againſt all Chriſtendome. Coming with an army of 1600000 men. (With portraits:—1. Emperour of Conſtantinople; 2. Emperour of Rome. In proſe.)

Wee alone the only Monarch, &c.

(No date.)

[*Vol.* ii. *p.* 1.

68.—. . . . of a Maid that was deep in Love with a Souldier brave and bold, Sir. (With illuſtration. Imperfect.)

To the tune of The Souldiers delight.

When first this Couple fill in Love.

Her Husband was a Musketeer, and she a famous Drummer (chorus).

No date.)

[*Vol.* ii. *p.* 2.

69.—Packingtons Pound.

When the Joy of all hearts, and desire of all eyes.

(No date.)

[*Vol.* ii. *p.* 3.

70.—A Defperate Combat between a Williamite Lady and a Jacobite.

In Yorkshire late happen'd a desperat Fight.

(No date.)

[*Vol.* ii. *p.* 4.

71.—Alas! for the Lofs of Cock-upps; or, Sarah Saywel, her Apology.

Upon a Night of misty Vapours.

(No date.)

[*Vol.* ii. *p.* 4.

72.—Love's Lamentable Tragedy. (With illuftration.)

To a pleasant new play house tune.

Tender Hearts of London City.

(No date.)

[*Vol.* ii. *p.* 5.

73.—The Courtly Triumph; or, an Excellent new Song upon the Coronation of K. William and Q. Marie; which was fplendidly celebrated on the 11th of April 1689.

To the tune of Cannons roar.

Sound the Trumpet, beat the Drum.

(No date.)

[*Vol.* ii. *p.* 6.

74.—An Excellent new Ballad, intituled, King William and his Forrester.

To its own proper tune.

You Subjects of Britain come listen a while.

(No date.)

[Vol. ii. p. 7.

75.—The Boon Companion; or, the Merry Loyal Boys of Suffolk's Jovitl (*sic*) Health. (With line of music.)

To the tune of Fond Boy.

We are the bold Suffolk boon revelling Boys.

London : Printed for C. Barnet, 1696.

[Vol. ii. p. 8.

76.—The True Englifh Prophet ; or, England's Happinefs a Hundred Years Hence.

To a new play-house tune.

Come chear up your Hearts, Boys, & all hands to Work.

A Hundred Years hence (chorus).

London : Printed for T. Alldridge in Southwark, 1697.

[Vol. ii. p. 9.

L.

77.—The Ladies of London's Petition; or, their Humble
        Addrefs to the Parliament of old Women for
        Hufbands: Sign'd by threefcore thoufand Hands,
        and never a crakt Maiden-head, nor widow amongft
        them.

> To the tune of Let Mary live long.

> *You Matrons all.*

> (No date. See No. 65.)

> [Vol. ii. p. 10.

78.—The Welfh-Mens Glory; or, the Famous Victories of the
        Antient Britans obtain'd upon St. David's Day.

> *The Honour, Glory, and the Grace.*

> London : Printed by Thomas Dawks, his Majesties
> British-Printer, at the West-End of Thames-
> Street. (No date.)

> [Vol. ii. p. 11.

79.—The Young Man's Wooing; or, a brief Defcription of
        the Properties of Widows and Laffes.

> To a pleasant new tune.

> *I once espy'd an handsome Wench.*

> (No date.)

> [Vol. ii. p. 12.

80.—The Life and Death of the Webſters Mare.

Tune of, To the Weaver when you.

In Brichin did a Webster dwell.

(No date.)

[*Vol.* ii. *p.* 13.

81.—The Weaver turn'd Devil; or, a New Copy of Verſes, on a Baker in Spitle-Fields, who was Frighted by a Weaver in the ſhape of a Devil. Shewing how the Baker went to Areſt the Weaver, for ſome Mony which he owed him for Bread.

To the tune of The Royal Foreſter.

You Bakers of England, both Country and Citty.

London: Printed for T. C., near Spitle-Fields, 1701.

[*Vol.* ii. *p.* 11.

82.—A Song on his Grace the Duke of Marlborough's happy Return into England; which is to be Sung this Day, being Thurſday the 23d of January 1707, by Mr. Abel, in the Tennis-Court.

Fame thy loudest blast prepare.

(No date.)

[*Vol.* ii. *p.* 15.

83.—The Glorious Warriour; or, a Ballad in Praise of General Stanhope. Dedicated to all who have Votes for Parliament-Men in the City of Weftminfter.

To the tune of Fair Rosamund.

When Anne, a Princess of Renown.

London: Printed for S. Popping, at the Black Raven in Paternofter-Row, 1710.

[Vol. ii. p. 16, 17

84.—The Jealous Weaver. (With illuftrations.)

A Weaver, Jealous of his Wife, like many.

(No date.)

[Vol. ii. p. 18.

85.—The Bifhop of Antioch, who was tempted by the Devil, in the likenefs of a Lady.

In Antioch fair Town.

(No date.)

[Vol. ii. p. 19.

86.—A Cheat in all Trads; or, the World turned upfid down. (With illuftrations.)

Good People now liften, I cannot forbear.

You may as well find a Needle in a Bottle of Hay (chorus).

No date.

[Vol. ii. p. 20

87.— . . . . paniards Defea . . . miral Vernon, Rear Admiral . . . ril laſt. Written by a Sailor on board . . . . (With illuſtration. Imperfect.)

Tune of Brave Vernon's Tryumph.

Once more, brave Boys, let us proclaim.

(No date.)

[*Vol.* ii. *p.* 21.

88.—Captain Kid's Farewel to the Seas; or, the Famous Pirate's Lament.

To the tune of Coming Down.

My Name is Captain Kid, who has sail'd.

(No date.)

[*Vol.* ii. *p.* 22.

89.—The Royal Strangers Ramble; or, the Remarkable Lives, Cuſtoms, and Character of the Four Indian Kings; with the manner of their Daily Paſtimes, Humours and Behaviours ſince their firſt Landing in England. Render'd into Pleaſant and Familiar Verse. Written by a Perſon of Quality.

Four Monarchs of Worth.

in Fetter-Lane, Fleet-street. 1710.

[*Vol.* ii. *p.* 2.

90.—Jockey and Jenney ; or, the Yiellding Maid overtaken. (With illuftrations.)

'Twas in the month of May, Jo.

(No date.)

[*Vol.* ii. *p.* 24.

91.—The Dame of Honour; or, Hofpitality. Sung by Mrs. Willis, in the Opera call'd The Kingdom of the Birds. (With illuftrations.)

Since now the world's turn'd upside down.

(No date.)

[*Vol.* ii *p.* 25.

92.—The Staffordfhire Maid. (With illuftrations.)

Come all ye young Gallants, and listen a while.

Printed and sold in Aldermary Church Yard, London. (No date.)

[*Vol.* ii. *p.* 26.

93.—Ralph and Nell's Ramble to Oxford (With illuftrations.)

I heard much talk of Oxford town.

Printed and Sold in Aldermary Church-Yard, Bow Lane, London. (No date.)

[*Vol.* ii. *p.* 27.

94.—(The fame Ballad. With different illuftrations.)

(Same imprint. No date.)

[*Vol.* ii *p.* 28.

95.—The Age of Man, displayed in Ten different Stages of Life. (With illustrations.)

In prime of Years, when I was Young.

Printed and Sold in Aldermary Church Yard, Bow Lane, London. (No date.)

[*Vol. ii. p. 29.*

96.—The Northern Lord. In Four Parts.

A Noble Lord of high renown.

Printed and sold in Aldermary Church-Yard, Bow Lane, London. (No date.)

[*Vol. ii. p. 30.*

97.—The Breath of Life; being an account of a Young Man that went to Sea, thinking it a pleasant Life; but soon found his Mistake. Prettily expressed in Sea Terms. (With illustration.)

When first I drew the Breath of Life.

(No date.)

[*Vol. ii. p. 31.*

98.—The Love-sick Serving-Man; shewing how he was wounded with the Charms of a Young Lady, but did not care to reveal his Mind. (With illustrations.)

E'er since I saw Clorinda's eyes.

Printed and Sold in Aldermary Church Yard, Bow Lane, London. (No date.)

[*Vol. ii. p. 32.*

99.—A True Relation of the Death of Sir Andrew Barton, a
    Pyrate and Rover.

When Flora with her fragrant flowers.

London : Printed and Sold at No. 4, Aldermary
Church Yard, Bow-Lane. (No date.)

[*Vol.* ii. *p.* 33.

100.—The Spanish Lady's Love to an English Sailor.   (With
    illustration.)

Will you hear of a Spanish Lady.

Printed and Sold in Aldermary Church-Yard, Bow
Lane, London. (No date.)

[*Vol.* ii. *p.* 34.

101.—Shepherd Adonis ; or, the Contented Lovers.   (With
    illustrations.)

Shepherd Adonis, being weary of his sport.

Printed and Sold at the Printing-Office, in Aldermary
Church-Yard, Bow-Lane, London. (No date.)

[*Vol.* ii. *p.* 35

102.—The Lady Isabella's Tragedy ; or, the Step Mother's
    Cruelty.   (With illustration.)

There was a Lord of worthy fame.

No date.)

[*Vol.* ii. *p.* 36.

F

107.—The Spanish Lady's Love to an English Captain. (With illuftrations.)

Will you hear of a Spanish lady.

Printed and Sold by J. Butler, High Street, Worcester. (No date.)

[*Vol.* ii. *p.* 41.

108.—The Cruel Step-Mother; or, the Unhappy Son.

You most indulgent parents lend an ear.

(No date.)

[*Vol.* ii. *p.* 42.

109.—The Penny worth of Wit. In Three Parts.

Here is a Penny Worth of Wit.

(No date.)

[*Vol.* ii. *p.* 43.

110.—The Four Indian Kings. In Two Parts. (With illuftrations.)

Attend unto a true relation.

(No date.)

[*Vol.* ii. *p.* 44.

111.—Sweet William of Plymouth.

A Seaman of Dover, Sweet William by name.

Printed and Sold in Bow Church-Yard. (No date.)

[*Vol.* ii. *p.* 45.

112.—Windfor Lady. (With illuftrations.)

To an excellent Northern tune.

In Windsor famous town did dwell.

Printed and Sold in Bow-church-yard, London
(No date.)

[*Vol.* ii. *p.* 46

113.—The Unhappy Memorable Song of the Hunting of Chevy Chafe. (With illuftration.)

God prosper long our noble King.

(No date.)

[*Vol.* ii *p.* 47.

114.—The Life and Death of Fair Rofamond, King Henry the Second's Concubine. (With illuftration.)

When as king Henry rul'd this land.

Printed and Sold in Bow-Church Yard, London.
(No date.)

[*Vol.* ii. *p.* 49.

115.—The King and Northern-Man; or, the Oppref'd Tennant Redref's'd.

To drive away the weary day.

(No date.)

[*Vol.* ii *p.* 49

116.—The Plymouth Tragedy ; or, Fair Sufan's Overthrow.
    (With illuftration.)

   Beautiful virgins of birth and breeding.

                        Printed and Sold at the Printing Office in Bow-
                            Church-Yard, London.   (No date.)

                                        [*Vol.* ii. *p.* 50.

117.—Patient Griffel.   An Excellent Ballad. (With illuftration.)

   A Noble Marquis, as he was hunting.

              (No date.)
                                        [*Vol.* ii. *p.* 51.

118.—The Cruel Knight, and the Fortunate Farmer's Daughter.

   In famous York city a farmer did dwell.

              (No date.)
                                        [*Vol.* ii. *p.* 52.

119.—A Pleafant Ballad of King Henry II. and the Miller of
    Mansfield ; fhewing how he was Entertain'd and
    Lodg'd at the Miller's Houfe.

   Henry our royal king would ride a hunting.

                        Printed and Sold at the Printing Office, in Bow-
                            Church-Yard, London.   (No date.)

                                        [*Vol.* ii. *p.* 53.

120.—A Choice Pennyworth of Wit.

Here is a Pennyworth of Wit.

Printed and Sold in Bow-Church Yard, London.
(No date.)
[*Vol.* ii. *p.* 54.

121.—Fair Maudlin, the Merchant's Daughter of Briftol.

Behold the touchstone of true love.

Printed and sold in Bow Church-Yard, London.
(No date.)
[*Vol.* ii. *p.* 55.

122.—The Humours of Rag-Fair; or, the Countryman's
defcription of their feveral Trades and Callings.
(With illuftration.)

Last Week in Lent I came to Town.

London: Printed and Sold in Stonecutter Street,
Fleet-Market. (No date.)
[*Vol.* ii. *p.* 56.

123.—Hunting of Chevy Chafe.

God prosper long our noble King.

Printed by Dunning, in Windsor. (No date.)
[*Vol.* ii. *p.* 57.

124.—The Kentifh Tragedy; or, Edward and Hannah. An
affecting Tale. (With illuftration.)

Beside a pleasant hill in Kent.

London: Printed and sold by J. and C. Evans,
Long-lane. (No date.)
[*Vol.* ii. *p.* 58.

125.—The Weavers and Clothiers Complaint againſt the Eaſt-India-Trade. Part I.

When first the Indian Trade began.

London : Printed, and are to be sold by A. Baldwin,
in Warwick-Lane, 1699.

[*Vol.* ii. *p.* 59.

126.—Four and Twenty Queries relating to the Eaſt-India Trade. Part II. (In profe.)

Since some very good Friends, &c.

London : Printed, and are to be Sold by A. Baldwin,
in Warwick-Lane, 1699.

[*Vol.* ii. *p.* 60.

127.—A New Advice to Whore-Maſters, &c.

O ! Scotland now repent.

(No date.)

[*Vol.* ii. *p.* 61.

128.—Woods and Groves and Ratling Streams ; or, the Lamentation of a Love-ſick Lady.

Sung with its own sweet air.

Ye Woods and Groves, and ratling Streams.

(No date.)

[*Vol.* ii. *p.* 62.

129.—An Excellen Balladt (*sic*), intituled, The Gaberlunzie-Man. (With illuſtration.)

The silly poor Man came o'er the Lee.

(No date.)

[*Vol.* ii. *p.* 63.

130.—The New Way of Gaberlunzy Man. (With illuſtrations.)

To its own proper tune.

Once in a Morning sweet and fair.

(No date.)

[*Vol.* ii. *p.* 64.

131.—An Excellent New Song, intituled, The New Way of "The laſt Time I came o're the Moor," &c.

To its own proper tune.

The last Time I came o're the Moor.

(No date.)

[*Vol.* ii. *p.* 65.

132.—Gilderoy.

To its own proper tune.

My Love he was as brave a Man.

(No date.)

[*Vol.* ii. *p.* 66.

133.—A Bonny Lafs for to ly with me.

To its own proper tune.

There lives a Lass on Eathing side.

(No date.)

[*Vol.* ii. *p.* 67.

134.—The Laird of Dyſarts Dreame.

I, the Laird of Dyſert, Melvine by name.

(No date.)

[*Vol.* ii. *p.* 68.

135.—The Laſt Words of James Mackpherſon, Murderer. (With illuſtration.)

I ſpent my time in rioting.

(No date.)

[*Vol.* ii. *p.* 69.

136.—The Gentle Montgomeries; an Excellent New Song, giving an Account of their Original, and of Rodger Earl of Montgomery, Salſberry and Arundale General to William the Conqueror his comming to England, with ſeveral Parts of Hiſtory concerning them, ending with an Advice to the Chief of the Clan.

To its own proper tune.

A Noble Roman was the Root.

(No date.)

[*Vol.* ii. *p* 70.

137.—A Lamentable Ballad of Fair Rosamond, Concubine to
Henry 2nd, who was put to death by Queen Eleanor,
in the famous Bower of Woodstock, near Oxford.
(With illustration.)

To the tune of Flying Fame.

When as King Henry rul'd the land.

Printed and Sold by J. Pitts, No. 14, Great Saint
Andrew Street, Seven Dials. Price One Penny.
(No date.)

[*Vol.* ii. *p.* 71.

138.—The Blind Beggar of Bethnal Green; shewing how his
Daughter was Married to a Knight, and had 3,000*l.*
to her Portion.

This song's of a beggar, who long lost his sight.

Printed and sold by Jennings, Water-lane, Fleet-
street, London. Price One Penny. (No date.)

[*Vol.* ii. *p.* 72.

139.—The Wanton Wife of Bath. (With illustration.)

In Bath a wanton wife did dwell.

Printed and Sold by J. Pitts, No. 14, Great St.
Andrew Street, 7 Dials. (No date.)

[*Vol.* ii. *p.* 73.

140.—The Cruel Cooper of Ratcliff. (With illustration.)

Near Ratcliff Cross liv'd a cooper there.

Printed and sold by J. Pitts, No. 14, Great st.
Andrew-street, seven Dials. Price One Penny.
(No date.)

[*Vol.* ii. *p.* 74.

141.—The Tragical Ballad of the Nobleman's Cruelty to his Son.

Both parents and lovers I pray now attend.

Printed and Sold by J. Pitts, No. 14, Great St. Andrew Street, Seven Dials. (No date.)

[*Vol. ii. p. 75.*

142.—Northamptonſhire Tragedy.

Young lovers lead an ear, I'm sure you'll shed a tear.

Printed and Sold by J. Pitts, 14, Great St. Andrew Street, Seven Dials. (No date.)

[*Vol. ii. p. 76.*

143.—The Hiſtory of Adanaæus. (A leaf of MS.)

[*Vol. ii. p. 77.*

144.—A Paraphraſe upon the Lords Prayer, and the Creed.

I. *If any be distrest, and faine would gather.*

II. *Since it be fit that I account should give.*

R. B.

London: Printed in the yeare 1641.

[*Vol. iii. p. 1.*

145.—An Elegie upon the Death of the Mirrovr of Magnanimity, the right Honourable Robert Lord Brooke, Lord Generall of the Forces of the Counties of Warwick and Stafford, who was flain by a Mufket fhot at the fiege of Liechfield, the fecond day of March, 1642.

Back blushing morne, to thine Eternoll bed.

(Ex opere (præsertim) HENRICI HARINGTONI, φιλολόγα).

London : Printed for H. O. Anno Dom. 1642.

[*Vol.* iii. *p.* 2.

146.—Pyms Juncto.

Truth I could chide you, Sirs, why how so late?

Oxford : Printed for Wil. Web, 1643.

[*Vol.* iii. *p.* 3.

147.—I. London's Warning-Peece, being the Common-Prayers Complaint. (Three poems.)

What shall I doe ; I am cast out of doore.

II. O YES, O YES, O YES.

If any man have found Law in a Declaration.

III. LONDON'S SACRIFICE.

Will nothing serve? will nothing else suffice?

Yorke : Printed by Stephen Buckley, 1643.

[*Vol.* iii. *p.* 4.

148.—The City.

Draw neere you factious Citizens, prepare.

Oxford: Printed for William Web, 1643.

[*Vol.* iii. *p.* 5

149.—A Funerall Elegie on the unfortunate death of that worthy Major Edward Grey, July 26, 1644. (With Anagram, Regard I die; and three other Anagrams.)

Sad Prodigy! Can famous valiant Grey.

Chronog. { stren VVs, & eXpert Vs / MaIor Grey / CaDIt & eXpdraVIt } 1644. J. A.

Printed at London for I. W. in the old Baylie, 1644.

[*Vol.* iii. *p.* 6

150.—I thanke you twice; or,
     The City courting their owne ruine,
     Thank the Parliament twice, for their treble undoing.

The Hierarchy is out of date.

O God a mercy Parliament (chorus).

MR. FINIS.

Mr An. Dom. 1647.

[*Vol.* iii. *p.* 7

151.—Pratle your pleafure (under the Rofe).

There is an old Proverb, which al the world knows.

MR. FINIS.

Mr. An. Dom. 1647.

[*Vol.* iii. *p.* 8.

152.—Cromwell's Panegyrick.

Shall Presbyterian bells ring Cromwels praise.

Χαρολόφιλος.

Printed in the Yeer 1647.

[*Vol.* iii. *p.* 9.

153.—An Elegie upon the much lamented Death of that Noble and Valiant Commander, the Right honourable the Earl of Tiveot, Governour of Tangiers. Slain by the Moors [3d May 1664].

Can Tiveot, Britain's glorious victime, dye.

BY JO. CROUCH, GENT.

London: Printed for Tho. Palmer, at the Crown in Westminster Hall, 1664.

[*Vol.* iii. *p.* 10.

154.—An Epicædium on the Death of Her moft Serene Majefty Henrietta Maria de Bourbon, Queen-Mother of England, and Daughter to the late moft Puiffant King Henry le Grand, King of France and Navarre, &c. Obiit 31 Auguft, MDCLXIX.

Reader, draw near, and offer thy Divine.

With Allowance. No date.

[*Vol.* iii. *p.* 11.

155.—The True Prefbyterian without Difguife ; or, a Character
of a Prefbyterians Ways and Actions. By Sir John
Denham, Knight.

A Presbyter is such a Monstrous thing.

London : Printed for J. B., 1680.

[*Vol.* iii. *p.* 12, 13.

156.—An Elegie upon the Truly Worthy, and ever-to-be
remembred Loyal Gentleman, Captain Will. Bedlow,
Englad's (*sic*) Deliverer, and the Scourge of Rome :
who Departed this Life on the 22 of this inftant
Auguft ; to the great Grief of all True Proteftants.
With an Account of his Pious End.

Alas! what sullen Fate has hence convey'd.

London : Printed for Langley Curtiss, 1680.

[*Vol.* iii. *p.* 14.

157.—A Congratulation of the Proteftant-Joyner to Anthony
King of Poland, upon his Arrival in the Lower
World.

Welcom, my Lord, unto these Stygian Plains.

London : Printed for N. Thompson, Anno Dom.
1683.

[*Vol.* iii *p.* 15 –18

158.—The King of Poland's Ghoſt ; or, a Dialogue betwixt Pluto and Charon, upon his Reception.

Hold Stygian Sculler, what hast brought me here ?

London : Printed for Jos. Hindmarsh, at the Black-Bull in Cornhill, 1683.

[*Vol.* iii. *p.* 19, 20.

159.—I. An Elegy on the Right Honourable Anthony Earl of Shaftſbury, who dyed on the 21st of January 1683.

The Busie Statesmen who by Toyls unblest.

EPITAPH.

Under this Stone does Sleeping lye
All that was Earth of Shaftsbury.

II. An Elegy on the Death of (the much to be lamented) Anthony K. of Poland.

The busie Toney, who by Toil unblest.

EPITAPH.

Under this Stone doth rotting lie
All th' Devil has left of S————y.

London : Printed Anno Domini MDCLXXXIII

[*Vol.* iii. *p.* 21.

160.—To His Royal Highnefs, at his Happy Return from
Scotland.　Written by a Perfon of Quality.

When all the Glories of Triumphant Rome.

London : Printed for W. Davis, 1682.

[*Vol.* iii. *p.* 22, 23.

161.—A New Poem, to condole the going away of his
Excellency the Ambaffador, from the Emperour of
Fez and Morocco, to his own Countrey.　By a perfon
of Quality.

Sir, my Muse bid you welcome when you come.

W. W.

(No date.)

[*Vol.* iii. *p.* 24, 25.

162.—A Satyr againft Brandy.　Written by Jo. Hains, as he
saith himfelf.

Farewell Damn'd Stygian Juice, who dost bewitch.

Printed for Jos. Hindmarsh, at the Black-Bull in
Cornhill, 1683.

[*Vol.* iii *p.* 26, 27.

163.—A Mornings Ramble ; or, Iflington Wells Burlefqt.
(Allufions made to Epfom Wells and Tunbridge
Springs.)

Sated with Love and Wine last Night.

London : Printed by George Croom, for the Author,
1684.

[*Vol.* iii. *p.* 28.

164.—More Lampoons.

I. THE HIEROGLIPHICK.

Come Painter take a Prospect from this Hill.

II. TO THE RESPECTIVE JUDGES.

Dignifi'd things, may I your haves implore.

Printed, 1688.

[*Vol.* iii. *p.* 29.

165.—I. A Dialogue between a Late Lord Major, and a Recorder. As alſo the Battle Royal between three Clergy-Men; which had been Printed ſooner had the Authour dar'd to Publiſh it.

Pray Mr. Recorder.

II. THE BATTLE ROYAL.

To the tune of, A Soldier and a Sailour.

A Dean and a Prebendary.

London: Printed in the Year 1698.

[*Vol.* iii. *p.* 30.

166.—A Satyr upon the French King; written by a Non-Swearing Parſon, and drop'd out of his Pocket at Samm's Coffee-Houſe.

And hast thou left Old Jemmy in the Lurch?

London: Printed for Will. Jac-about, in the Year of Peace. (No date.)

[*Vol.* iii. *p.* 31. 32.

167.—Tho. Brown's Recantation of his Satyr on the French King.

And has this Bitch my Muse trapan'd me?

London: Printed, and are to be Sold by most Booksellers in London and Westminster, MDCXCVII.

[*Vol.* iii. *p.* 33, 34.

168.—Advice to the Kentifh Long-Tails, by the Wife-Men of Gotham. In Anfwer to their late Sawcy Petition to the Parliament. (Signed by the Mayor, &c., 12th of May.)

We, the Long-Heads of Gotham, &c.

London: Printed in the Year 1701.

[*Vol.* iii. p. 35.

169.—The Proteftant Queen; or, the Glorious Proclaiming her Royal Highnefs Princefs Ann of Denmark, Queen of England, Scotland, France, and Ireland, on the 8th of March 1702. To the joy and Satisfaction of all Loyal and Loving Subjects. (With illuftrations.)

To the tune of Gallant Sailor.

I must confefs that we all Lamented.

(No date.)

[*Vol.* iii. p. 36.

170.—An Elegy upon the Death of the Famous Dr. John Partridgd (*sic*), the Great Aftrologer, who departed this Life (according to Efq. Biggerftaff's Prediction) this Morning between the Hours of One and Two a Clock, being the 29th of March, at his Houfe near Covent-Garden. (With illuftration.)

O Partridge! Art thou gone, and we in Tears!

London : Printed in the Year 1708.

[*Vol.* iii. *p.* 37.

171.—A Hymn to the Pillory.

Hail Hi·eroglyphick State Machin.

(No date.)

[*Vol.* iii. *p.* 38 —41.

172.—A Satyr againft Mankind. Written by a Perfon of Honour.

Were I, who to my cost, already am.

(No date.)

[*Vol.* iii. *p.* 42 — 43.

173.—The Converts.

I did intend in Rhimes Heroick.

No date.)

174.—The Character of an Englifh-Man.

By the first Principles, of Mother Earth.

I have perused these Verses, and find them composed according to the Rules of Poetry, and therefore think them fitting to be Printed.

NATH. LEE.

(No date.)

[*Vol.* iii. *p.* 47, 48.

175.—The Parliaments Knell.

Farewell old Parliament of seaven yeares standing.

MR. FINIS.

(No date.)

[*Vol.* iii. *p.* 49.

176.—The Poor Poets Petition to the New Parliament.

Whereas, Conformists, & Dissenters.

(No date.)

[*Vol.* iii. *p.* 50, 51.

177.—I. The Cities Loyalty to their King.

Why kept your Train-bands such a stirre.

London is a brave Towne (chorus).

II. The 11. Members Iuftification.

Den. Hollis is a gallant man.

The Parliament hath sitten close (chorus).

(No date.)

[*Vol.* iii. *p.* 52.

178.—The Souldiers fad Complaint.

Is this the upshot then? We that have spent.

Per I. H.

(No date.)

[*Vol.* iii. *p.* 53.

179.—The Quaker's Song. Sung by Mrs. Willis, at the Theatre in Lincolns-Inn-Fields.

Amongst the pure Ones all, which Conscience doth profess.

(No date)

[*Vol.* iii. *p.* 54.

180.—The Sence of the Oxford-Iunto, concerning the late Treaty ; wherein the feverall Reafons are delivered, why they could not conclude a Peace with the Parliament : And Publifhed for the Satisfaction of the whole Kingdome.

Give eare (beloved Countrimen).

(No date.)

[*Vol.* iii. *p.* 55.

181.—To the High Court of Parlament, John Cragge doth his Requeft prefent.

(In the form of an acroftic.)

T—O You Right Worthies, worthy of Renowne.

No date.

[*Vol.* iii. *p.* 56.

182.—Irelands Complaint of the Armies hypocrifie. With his Excellencies entring unconquer'd London. In a Difcourfe between two freinds Donatus and Perigrin. With the flighting of the Communicable Line.

Well met friend Perigrin, from whence cam'st thou?

(No date.)

[*Vol.* iii. *p.* 57.

183.—The Publick Faith.

Some tell of Affrick Monsters, which of old.

(No date.)

[*Vol.* iii. *p.* 58.

184.—Troy-Novant muft not be Burnt ; or, an exhortative to the City to preferve themfelves.

What is there none that will the City right?

(No date.)

[*Vol.* iii. *p.* 59.

185.—An Eligie upon the univerfally-lamented Death of the thrice Noble and Vertuous Prince, Henry Duke of Gloucefter.

And is his breath expir'd? hath His Chaste Soul?

London : Printed for Thomas Parkhurft, at the lower end of Cheapside. (No date.)

[*Vol.* iii. *p.* 60.

186.—Lampoons.

 I. Over the Lord D——rs Door.

  Unhappy Age, and we in it.

 II. Over the Lord S——rys Door.

  If Cecil the Wise.

 III. To the Speaking-Head.

  I'm come my future Fate to seek.

 IV. The Ghost.

  A Papist dy'd, as 'twas Jehovah's Will.

 V. A Dialogue between a Loyal Addressor, and a Blunt Whiggish Clown.

  Ungrateful Wretch! Canst thou pretend a cause.

   (No date.)

        [Vol. iii. p. 61.

187.—St. James's, Jan. 1, 17⅛.—The following Address, from the Hundreds of Drury, was this Day presented to his Majesty by Mr. Cibber, introduced by his Grace the Duke of Newcastle, Lord Chamberlain of the Houshold; which Address his Majesty received very graciously.—To the King's Most Excellent Majesty, &c.

  Sir, Since the Scum of these three Nations.

   No date.)

        [Vol. iii. p. 62.

188.—The Sorrowful Lamentation of Counſellor Layer's, who was Condemned to die at London for High Treaſon.

Noble Hearts all round the Nation.

(No date.)

[Vol. iii. p. 63.

189.—The Confinement of the Seven Biſhops.

Where is there Faith or Justice to be found ?

(No date.)

[Vol. iii. p. 64

190.—An Elegy on the much lamented Death of Thomas Jekyll, D.D., Chaplain in Ordinary to His Majeſty, and Preacher at the New Chapel in Weſtminſter, who departed this Life on Sunday the 2d. of this Inſtant October.

His Prayr's at last are heard, and Heav'n has gain'd.

(No date.)

[Vol. iii. p. 65.

191.—Peg Trim Tram in the Suds ; or, No French Strolers. A New Ballad.

I sing you a Song, of a right noble ——.

Derry Down, Down (chorus).

(No date.)

[Vol. iii. p. 66

192.—Upon the Stately Structure of Bow-Church and Steeple ;
  Burnt, An. 1666 ; Rebuilt, 1679 ; or, a Second
  Poem upon Nothing.

  Look how the Country-Hobbs with wonder flock.

  (No date.)

  [*Vol.* iii. *p.* 67.

193.—Pimlico Aſſociation.—A Copy of Verſes spoken by
  Mr. R. Palmer, at the Celebration of the Anniverſary
  of her Majeſty's Birth-day, January 18th, 1799.

  Amid these scenes of war that round us rise.

  (No date.)

  [*Vol.* iii. *p.* 68.

194.—(No Title. Illuſtration of an Orator in a Waggon.)

  From how many Posts in King George's Dominions.

  (No date.)

  [*Vol.* iii. *p.* 69.

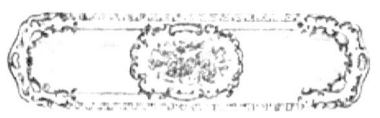

www.ingramcontent.com/pod-product-compliance
Lightning Source LLC
Chambersburg PA
CBHW030015030726
47499CB00008B/3010

9 7 8 3 7 4 4 7 7 7 0 8 7